W9-BZU-426

Four Fables from Aesop

Amy Lowry

Holiday House / New York

To Larry,
my favorite Fox

Printed and Bound in November 2011 at Kwong Fat Offset Printing Co., Ltd., Dongguan City, China.
The text typeface is McKracken.
The illustrations were done with gouache and pencil
on cold press 100% cotton paper.
www.holidayhouse.com
First Edition
1 3 5 7 9 10 8 6 4 2

Library of Congress Cataloging-in-Publication Data
Lowry, Amy.
Fox tails : four fables from Aesop / Amy Lowry. —1st ed.
p. cm.
Summary: Four of Aesop's fables are combined in this tale about
three animal friends who outsmart a tricky fox.
ISBN 978-0-8234-2400-9 (hardcover)
[1. Fables. 2. Folklore.] I. Aesop. II. Title.
PZ8.2.L76Fo 2012
398.24'52—dc23
[E]
2011027718

The fox was cranky. He had slept through breakfast, and his stomach growled. He padded over to the refrigerator. It was empty. "Drat," he muttered.

The fox remembered seeing some grapes near the end of the lane. "Hmmmm," he thought. "Those grapes would be perfect for my lunch."

He hurried down the path; and sure enough, he spotted a bunch of large, green grapes. They were hanging from a vine, which trailed over a high branch.

He took a step back and, with great effort, ran toward the tree and leaped up in the air, just missing the grapes. Turning around, he tried again, and again, and again, until he landed hard on the ground.

"Well," he said, dusting himself off. "I thought those grapes were ripe, but I can see now that they are quite sour." He stuck his nose high in the air and resumed his walk.

Presently he came to a crow sitting in a tree with a large piece of Swiss cheese in her mouth.

The fox gazed at the crow. "Well, well," he said. "This must be my lucky day. Has anyone ever told you how beautiful you are?" The crow gazed back. "Black is a good color on you. And your feathers really sparkle in the sunlight."

The crow was very flattered and stretched out her wings so that the fox could get a better view.

"You know," said the fox. "I've heard it said that out of all the birds, you have the most amazing voice. Is that true?"

The crow could barely contain herself. She lifted her head and began to caw; but the moment she opened her mouth . . . the cheese fell to the ground and was quickly gobbled up by the fox.

“In exchange for your cheese, madam,” he said, “I will give you a piece of advice. Never trust a flatterer.” With that he resumed his walk down the lane.

The fox was so busy congratulating himself that he failed to see the empty well that lay just ahead. Before he knew it, he plunged headlong into a small, stinky, dark hole.

"Drat," he muttered. He tried to climb up the side of the well, but it was slippery and coated with moss.

Presently, he heard the jingle jangle of a bell, and soon enough he saw a goat peering down at him. The goat was thirsty and asked the fox if the water was good.

"Good?" said the fox. "Why, it's the best water I have ever tasted."

The goat, who could think of nothing but quenching his thirst, jumped in at once. When he had had enough to drink, he looked about, like the fox, for some way of getting out but could find none.

The fox turned to the goat. “I have an idea,” he said. “You stand up on your hind legs and plant your forelegs against the side of the well. I’ll climb up on your back. Once I’m out, I can help you out too!”

The goat quickly agreed, and the fox climbed onto his back and hoisted himself out of the well. Pleased with himself, he began to walk away.

"Wait," cried the goat. "You promised to help me!"

The fox stopped and replied, "Look before you leap next time!"

And without looking back, the fox headed home for his afternoon nap.

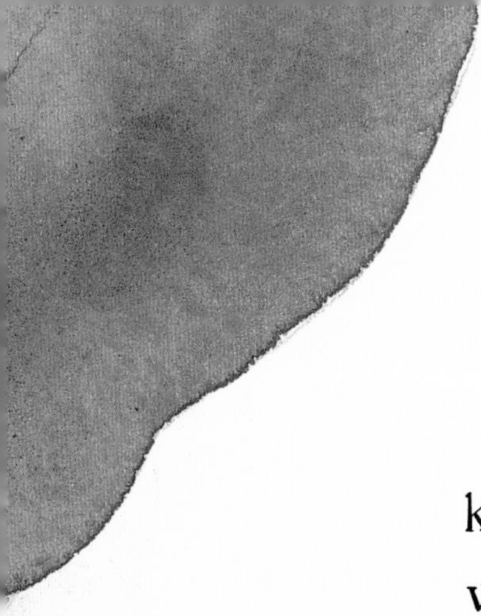

The goat was in the well for several hours before a kind farmer helped him out. He trotted down the lane, where he ran into the crow.

They shared their misadventures with Mr. Fox and together decided to seek revenge. "But how?" The crow sighed.

"I know how," said a voice from behind the hedge. The crow and the goat looked around and saw a large white stork standing by the road.

She proceeded to tell them of a dinner she had recently eaten at the fox's house.

COOKIE
ANANSI TALES
TRICKSTER TALES
OMELETTES
CHICKEN RECIPES
FOXX
VOLPONE
Pickle
EGG
GRA
X
BONE MEAL

"I was hungry," she said, "and the food smelled delicious. He had made lentil soup—one of my favorites! I sat down and was looking forward to a good meal. But that trickster fox served the soup in a saucer. I could barely get a drop on the end of my bill. I was helpless, while he lapped up the entire bowlful."

The stork paused. "I've invited the fox to dinner tonight," she continued. "Come and see how it goes."

The goat and the crow followed the stork back to her home, where they hid in the pantry and waited for the fox to arrive.

Soon after there was a knock at the door.

"Come in," said the stork. "I've made some delicious fish stew."

The fox was quite hungry after his busy day and sat down at the table. The stork carefully ladled the stew into two tall jars with very narrow necks.

She brought them to the table, sat down, and proceeded to dip her long beak into the jar. The fox tried to insert his snout, but the rim was too narrow. All he could manage to do was lick the outside of the jar. It was a very silly sight.

The goat and the crow were soon rolling on the floor with laughter. When the fox realized he had been tricked, he flew into a rage and stalked out of the house.

"Drat," he muttered, and headed home to bed hungry.

The stork shook her head. "Serves him right," she said, and went into the kitchen. She returned with two deep bowls. "Please," she said, "stay and join me for supper."

The three sat down and shared the stew, which was indeed delicious.

AUTHOR'S NOTE

A fable is a story or poem intended to reveal a useful observation called a moral. The characters in fables are most often talking animals that act like humans but keep some of their animal traits. Throughout history, fables have been a popular method of teaching lessons. The four fables woven into a story in this book have been attributed to Aesop, a slave and storyteller who is believed to have lived in ancient Greece more than 2,500 years ago. His fables were kept alive through the art of storytelling. They have been told and retold in many different languages and have reached countless generations. The first printed version of Aesop's fables in English appeared in 1484.

Like all of Aesop's fables, each of the four in this book ends with a moral:
THE FOX AND THE GRAPES: It is easy to scorn what you cannot get.
THE FOX AND THE CROW: Never trust a flatterer.
THE FOX AND THE GOAT: Look before you leap.
THE FOX AND THE STORK: One bad turn deserves another.